Bother with Boris

Bother with Boris

Diana White

Text and illustrations copyright © 1989 Diana White

First published in Great Britain in 1989 by ABC

This edition first published in 1991 by softbooks,
an imprint of ABC, All Books for Children,
a division of The All Children's Company Ltd
10 Museum Street, London WC1A 1JS

Printed and bound in China

British Library Cataloguing in Publication Data
White, Diana
Bother with Boris.
I. Title
823.914 [J]

ISBN 1-85704-002-3

For Matthew and Adam

"Time you had a bath,"
said Mrs Polar Bear.

"Shan't,"
said Boris.

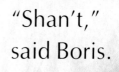

The bath had two taps.
One said COLD and the other said COLDER.

"Your bath is ready now,"
said Mrs Bear.
She threw in a pawful of ice-cubes.

"Mothers are always telling you to get into baths,"
grumbled Boris.

"And this bathroom's too hot,"
he muttered.

Mrs Bear opened wide the window
so the snow could blow in.

"Would you like your penguin in the bath with you?"
asked Mrs Bear.
The penguin's name was Biscuit.

"My friends like me with dirty fur,"
said Boris,

and he crawled under the bath.

"When you're clean you can have a fish lolly,"
promised Mrs Bear.

But Boris meant to go on sulking for hours and hours.

". . . and a plate of fish fingers
as tall as an iceberg,"
said Mrs Bear.
"Well . . . . ,"
said Boris.

" . . . and a slice of Igloo cake."

"Can I chase the Eskimos afterwards?"
asked Boris.

"Last time their husky chased you,
you hid under my fur all night,"
said Mrs Bear.

Biscuit laughed rather a lot,

and Boris looked very cross.

Boris and Biscuit played their special snowball game in the bath.

Each scored when a snowball hit his friend on the nose.
Boris kept score.

"Time to dry yourselves,"
said Mrs Bear.

She fetched two towels from the fridge.

"Hurry up, or the water will be getting warm."

"Mothers are always telling you to get out of baths,"
grumbled Boris.

Boris had a plate of fish fingers
stacked high as an iceberg,
two slices of Igloo cake,
bearberry jam,

a fish lolly, and a cup of tea with
three spoonfuls of crushed ice.
Biscuit had seaweed salad
and all the sardines.

"Time you went to bed,"
said Mrs Polar Bear,

as she brought Boris his cold water bottle.

"Clean your teeth first, Boris.
Remember, polar bears have the best teeth
of all the animals,"

she said, as she left him in the bathroom.

Boris picked up his tube of Frostadent.

But instead of squeezing it on his toothbrush,
he drew a picture of himself

all over the bathroom mirror,

and under it he wrote

BORIS IS THE BEST